Ginger
the Stray
Kitten

Ginger
the Stray
Kitten

Holly Webb

Illustrated by Sophy Williams

SCHOLASTIC INC.

New York Toronto London Auckland
Sydney Mexico City New Delhi Hong Kong

For Sophie

ISBN: 978-0-545-23279-1

12 11 10 9 8 7 6 5 4 3 2 1   10 11 12 13 14 15/0

Printed in the U.S.A.
First Scholastic printing, January 2010

Chapter One

"Can we stop by the farm today?" Rosie asked her grandma hopefully. They had a few different ways back from school to Gran's house, but the road past the farm was Rosie's favorite. That was the good thing about Gran picking her up from school while Mom was at work. Gran wasn't usually in a rush, and she didn't mind walking slowly while Rosie stopped to look at any cats she happened to meet along the way. Rosie loved cats and was desperate for one of her own, but she hadn't managed to persuade her mom yet.

Gran smiled at her. "Oh, I suppose we could go home that way. I could pick up some eggs from Mrs. Bowen. I might make a cake tonight, for the weekend." She looked down at Rosie and said thoughtfully, "But you know how she likes to chat, Rosie. Are you sure you won't get bored?"

Rosie looked up at her in surprise, and realized that Gran was teasing. Gran knew that Rosie loved going to the farm, because while she was talking to Mrs. Bowen, Rosie could go watch the stray cats in the farmyard.

There were a lot of them, and Gran said they were called feral cats because they weren't anyone's pets. Rosie had never managed to count them all, because they were so hard to see, but she thought there were probably about twenty of them. Mrs. Bowen put food out occasionally, but mostly they lived on the mice they caught in the barns.

Rosie loved to imagine that the cats belonged to her, but they weren't really very friendly. If she sat on the foot step of the old rusty tractor for a while, they might prowl past her, but they wouldn't let her pet them.

One of the prettiest cats, a tabby with beautiful spots, had given birth to a litter of kittens about five weeks before. Rosie had heard them meowing in the barn, but she hadn't been able to see them, as the tabby cat had hidden them under some old hay bales that were stored in there.

Now the kittens were all running around the farmyard, and they weren't quite as shy as the older cats. Rosie was really hoping that she could tame one of them. She dreamed of taking a kitten home as a pet of her own.

She knew which one she wanted most of all—the gorgeous little ginger boy kitten. He was so sweet—he had gingery-creamy fur with darker orange stripes, and an amazingly bright pink nose. His eyes were very green and very big, and Rosie thought he was the most handsome cat she'd ever seen.

Sometimes people called Rosie Ginger because of her long, curly red hair. Mom had always told her that her red hair was beautiful and different, and that she'd like it when she was older, but Rosie wasn't so sure. Then she had seen the kitten. She felt like she and the kitten were a pair, with their ginger coloring. They were ginger and proud of it!

She wished the ginger kitten would let her stroke him. She could just imagine how soft his fur would be. The other day he'd actually come close enough to sniff at her fingers, but he'd darted off again without letting Rosie touch him.

Gran called hello at Mrs. Bowen's

back door, which was half open, and Rosie looked eagerly around the farmyard. She had something special for the cats today, and she was really hoping she could tempt the ginger kitten to come over to her. Rosie had noticed at lunch that her friend Millie had a ham sandwich. Mom usually put peanut butter sandwiches in Rosie's lunch box, because they were her favorite, but she couldn't help thinking that the kitten would love

Millie's sandwich because the ham smelled delicious. Millie was picking at the ham with a bored expression.

"Don't you like your sandwich?" Rosie asked, a plan starting to form in the back of her mind.

"I wanted peanut butter, but my brother used it all," Millie sighed. "I hate ham. . . ."

"Do you want to trade? I've only got half left, but it's peanut butter," Rosie offered hopefully.

"You sure?" Millie looked delighted. "I didn't know you liked ham. You can have the whole thing!"

Rosie had slowly eaten half of the sandwich, and then tucked the other one away in her lunch box.

"Didn't you like it?" Millie asked.

Rosie leaned over closer to her. The kitten felt like a special secret, and she didn't want everyone to know. "I'm saving it. Remember the gorgeous ginger kitten I was telling you about that lives on the farm on the way back to my gran's house? He came right up to me the other day, and I bet if I had some food, he might even let me pet him. You don't mind, do you?"

Millie shook her head. "Of course not! Oh, you're so lucky, going to see kittens. Are they tiny?"

."The lady who owns the farm thinks they're about five weeks old. They're so cute! Maybe your mom would let you come home with us and see them one day? I'm sure Gran wouldn't mind. You could stay for dinner."

Now Rosie carefully unwrapped Millie's sandwich and started to crumble it into little bits, very gently, trying to keep as still and quiet as she could. It didn't take long for the cats to get a whiff of the delicious, meaty smell.

Rosie caught a movement out of the corner of her eye, just a streak of black fur. It was one of the kittens, popping its head around the tractor wheel, trying to see what that yummy smell was. Suddenly, several more little cat faces popped up, their whiskers twitching as they sniffed the air.

Rosie threw a piece of sandwich on the ground a little way away, and the closest kitten, the black one, pounced and swallowed it whole. Then he looked up for more. All the other kittens padded a few steps forward, not wanting to miss out. This time Rosie dropped the food closer, and one of the tabby kittens darted in and grabbed it, running back to a safe distance before she dared to stop and eat.

Rosie's heart thumped with delight as she saw her favorite ginger kitten patter across the farmyard, eager to join in. She tried to throw the next piece close to him, but the tabby kitten got there first and gobbled it up, right under his nose. The ginger kitten gave Rosie a helpless look. *I'm so hungry*, he seemed to be saying. *Pllleeeease feed me. . . .*

This time Rosie threw him an extra-large piece. The ginger kitten held it down with one paw and hissed when the others circled around him. Rosie

laughed out loud—his furious little face was so funny—and the kittens looked up at her in shock, their eyes wide. Then they all shot off back into their hiding places. "Oh, no!" Rosie muttered to herself, wishing she hadn't been so noisy.

But the ginger kitten had only run a couple of steps away from his piece of sandwich, and now he eyed it uncertainly. Food—but also a noisy girl. What was he supposed to do? He eyed her thoughtfully. He'd seen her before; she came quite often. She didn't usually make noise, and she was quiet now. She wasn't even moving. And she still had lots more of that sandwich.

He darted over and gulped down the

rest of his piece, then looked around. His brother and sisters were hiding still. If he went closer, while they weren't here, he might get *more* sandwich. . . . Nervously, ready to run in case she made that loud noise again, he edged closer, his eyes on the ham.

Rosie carefully tossed him a little piece, much nearer to her feet this time.

The kitten stared at her suspiciously. Rosie looked back. Maybe it was too close. But then the kitten moved one paw forward cautiously, and then the other, and then he was just close enough. He started to gobble the sandwich, with one eye on Rosie all the time.

When it was all gone, he sat up and eyed her hopefully, licking his whiskers. He cast a quick look behind him. The others were all watching, but they weren't coming any closer. The food was all his! He knew it was risky, but the sandwich was too delicious. He had to have more!

Rosie couldn't help smiling. He was only a few inches away from her foot, almost close enough to touch. This time, instead of throwing the sandwich, she just held out her hand with the last few pieces in it.

The ginger kitten stared at her nervously. What was he supposed to do now? The smell of that sandwich was so good. He could just run up and grab it, couldn't he? He skittered forward, his whiskers trembling, and quickly licked up a few crumbs from Rosie's hand, before stepping back to watch her again.

Then he heard a noise and looked around. His brother and sisters were starting to creep closer! They'd seen that he wasn't afraid, so they were getting braver, too. If he didn't wolf that sandwich down fast, he might have to share it.

The ginger kitten hurried back to Rosie and started to eat as fast as he could, licking the crumbs away with his rough little tongue. Rosie had to try hard not to giggle—he was tickling her!

In a few seconds the kitten had eaten it all. He glared at her hand, obviously wondering when it was going to produce some more.

"Sorry, it's all gone," Rosie whispered. "But I'll bring you some more next time. I bet Mom would let me have ham sandwiches if I asked, and I'd give them all to you."

The kitten eyed her expectantly, and Rosie stretched out her hand. He licked it, but there was no more ham.

Rosie gently stroked the top of his head, and he jumped in surprise, looking up at her with enormous emerald eyes. *What was that for?* he seemed to be saying. Rosie guessed he just wasn't used to being petted. He didn't know that she was trying to be nice. It made Rosie feel sad.

"Rosie! Where are you?" It was Gran, calling from the farmhouse door. The ginger kitten raced for the safety of the barn at top speed, chasing after his brother and sisters, and Rosie sighed as she got up. Still, she had managed to pet him! That was a first. He was so little and thin, but his fur had been gorgeously soft, exactly as she'd imagined. More than ever, Rosie wished she could have a kitten just like him. . . .

Chapter Two

Rosie thought about the ginger kitten all weekend. It was such a big step that he'd let her pet him! Maybe she really would be able to tame him. He was very young, after all.

She sat dreamily at the kitchen table drawing pictures of the kitten, while Mom was writing a shopping list. It was so hard to get his stripes right, she had to keep starting again.

"That's beautiful, Rosie!" Mom said, leaning over.

Rosie shook her head. "His face should be more of a peachy color. I don't have the right marker for it."

"Is it a real cat?" Mom asked. "One of the ones you see on the way home from school?"

"He's a kitten at Mrs. Bowen's farm," Rosie explained. "You know, the little farm down the road, about two minutes' walk from Gran's house? There's five of them altogether. You'd love them, Mom."

She looked hopefully at her mother. Maybe if Mom came and saw how cute the kittens were, she'd let them take the little ginger one home. If only Rosie could tame him . . .

"He does look cute," her mom agreed. "Just be careful, though. Those wild cats have probably got all sorts of disgusting bugs."

Rosie sighed. That didn't sound particularly hopeful. . . .

Rosie's mom couldn't understand why she was so anxious to get to school on Monday morning.

"I'm going to be at work early, at this rate," she said. "What's gotten into you, Rosie? Usually it's me telling you to get a move on."

Rosie just smiled. The sooner she was at school, the sooner it would be over and she could persuade Gran to take her to the farm again. Or it felt that way, anyway, even though she knew that really it didn't make any difference how early she got there.

She'd made sure Mom bought ham for her sandwiches this week, and she'd begged for an extra yogurt so she could save each sandwich and not have her tummy rumbling all afternoon.

Luckily, Gran didn't mind going to the farm again and chatting with Mrs. Bowen. Rosie ran ahead as they went down the road that led past the farm, calling to her gran to hurry.

"I can't walk any faster, Rosie," said Gran. "You really do love those cats, don't you?" She was frowning a little as she said it, but Rosie was thinking about whether the ginger kitten would remember her and didn't notice.

It seemed to Rosie that the cats appeared more quickly this time when she sat down on the old tractor. Obviously they remembered her as the food person. The ginger kitten was the first to appear, his wide, white whiskers twitching with anticipation. Rosie wished he wasn't so nervous around her and that she could take him home and look after him. She crumbled the sandwich and scattered a few pieces around, hoping that again he'd be brave enough to come really close.

The kitten happily sniffed the air. More ham! And the others weren't as brave as he was, so he could have most of it to himself. He was sure the girl wasn't dangerous—she *had* touched him last time, but very gently. It had been quite nice. He would even let her pet him again, if there was ham.

Rosie watched hopefully as he crept forward, and she held out a particularly yummy-looking piece of ham. The kitten nibbled it delicately, then bumped her hand with his forehead, as if to say thank you. Rosie held out her left hand with some more sandwich, and carefully rubbed behind his ears with the other.

The kitten looked up at her, still confused about why she wanted to pet him like this, but not minding too much. He even purred, just a little. He was a bit itchy behind the ears, and she was rubbing exactly the right spot.

He finished the last of the sandwich and stared at Rosie, sniffing her fingers to see if more food would appear. When it didn't, he yawned, showing a very pink tongue, and jumped on his little tabby sister's tail, starting a kitten wrestling match.

Rosie watched them, giggling

quietly to herself. They were so funny! Maybe tomorrow she would bring a piece of string for them to chase—she was sure they would like that.

The kittens suddenly scattered, and Rosie turned to see her gran coming out of the farmhouse and waving good-bye to Mrs. Bowen. Gran looked worried, and Rosie jumped up.

"What's the matter?" she asked as

they headed out the gate.

Gran looked down at her and sighed. "I've been meaning to talk to you about this for a while, Rosie," she said. "Mrs. Bowen is moving—she's going to live with her son. The farmhouse is too big for her now that she's on her own."

Rosie stared up at Gran in surprise. She couldn't imagine the farm without Mrs. Bowen. "Oh. . . . So who's going to live at the farm now?" she asked. "Is Mrs. Bowen selling it?" Rosie looked back at the farm gate. There was no FOR SALE sign up.

"No . . ." Gran hesitated. "Well, yes, I suppose she is. The land has been sold to a developer—they're going to knock down the farm buildings and put up some houses instead. Mrs. Bowen signed the contract with them a little while ago, and she's been gradually packing her things up and moving them over to her son's house. She's leaving the farm this week."

Rosie gasped. It was all happening so quickly. Then a horrible thought struck her. "But Gran, what's going to happen to the cats? They won't stay around when the farm's a construction site! Where will they go?"

"It's all right, Rosie," Gran said soothingly, putting an arm around her shoulders. "Mrs. Bowen's asked the people from the Animal Rescue Center in Wilmerton to find the cats a home. They're going to come and collect them tomorrow, she told me. It'll be much better for the cats, you know. They'll check them over, and find good homes for the kittens. As for the older cats, they'll try and find someone with farm buildings or stables who'll have them as outdoor cats, like they are here."

Rosie nodded. "But I won't see them anymore," she said sadly, her voice quivering. "Not even the little ginger kitten, and he was starting to like me, Gran, he really was. I . . . I even thought of trying to take him home, if I could convince Mom. . . ."

"I'm not surprised he liked you, considering you were feeding him all your sandwiches." Gran smiled at her. "Mrs. Bowen does have windows and I'm not blind, Rosie!"

"Oh." Rosie looked up at Gran, her cheeks a little pink. "You won't tell Mom, will you?" she asked.

"Well, no. But I think you'd have been better off eating the sandwiches yourself and buying some cat treats with your allowance," Gran suggested.

"I don't think your mother would like to know she was making sandwiches for a tribe of wild cats."

"It won't matter now, anyway," Rosie said tearfully. "I'll never see any of them again!"

When Mom picked Rosie up from Gran's that night, she was surprised by the quiet, sad little figure who trailed down the stairs.

"What's up, Rosie? Did you have a bad day at school?" she asked.

Rosie shook her head.

"You go get your things, Rosie," Gran suggested, and by the time Rosie had packed up her homework and her pencil case, Gran had obviously told Mom what was going on, because she didn't ask again.

Rosie stared miserably out of the car window as they drove back to their house, which was a few miles away from Gran's. The rescue center people would be thinking about new homes for the kittens already, she supposed. All of those lucky people who'd be getting gorgeous kittens. Rosie wondered who would get to adopt the ginger kitten. Maybe there'd be a girl her age. But she was sure no one would ever love him as much as she did. She was so jealous.

Suddenly, Rosie sat up straight, staring out of the front window in excitement. Why shouldn't that girl be her? The kitten needed a new home, and he already liked her. She could name him Ginger! It was perfect!

Except that she would have to convince her mom, of course.

"What is it, Rosie?" her mom asked. "A rabbit didn't run in front of the car, did it? I didn't feel anything."

"What? No! Mom, can we have a kitten?" Rosie babbled. "Please? All of Mrs. Bowen's cats need new homes, and we'd be a perfect new home, wouldn't we?"

Mom didn't say anything for a minute, and Rosie stared at her hopefully. At least she hadn't said no right away.

"I don't know, Rosie," Mom murmured at last. "It would be nice to have a pet—but those kittens are wild.

They aren't used to people. I don't know if we'd be the right home. Someone who knows more about cats would be better, I think."

"We could learn about cats!" Rosie pointed out eagerly. "And those kittens really, really need homes, Mom. Did Gran tell you the rescue center people are coming to get the cats tomorrow? They'll hate being in a shelter, in cages. There's one of the kittens, Mom, he's really sweet, and he's already almost tame. He lets me pet him and he even eats out of my hand. He'd be a fantastic pet!"

"Well, I'll think about it. Maybe we could go see them, see how tame they really are. I'm not sure I want a wild kitten climbing my curtains. . . ."

Rosie beamed. She was sure that Ginger was hers already. He was so cute that Mom just wouldn't be able to resist him!

Back at the farm, the ginger kitten curled up next to his mother and brother and sisters, in a pile of hay in the old barn. It made a cozy nest, and he licked his paw sleepily. He was thinking about that girl and wondering if she would come back tomorrow. She might bring more food, and maybe she would pet his fur again. It was nice when she did that, like his mother licking his ears.

He snuggled up closer to his tabby

sisters and closed his eyes. The hay was soft and warm, and he quickly fell asleep, never dreaming that everything was about to change.

Chapter Three

The next morning, the kittens were startled awake by the noise of a vehicle driving into the yard. Mrs. Bowen didn't have a car, and she took most of her eggs to the village shop to sell, so very few people drove up to the farm. The kittens blinked at one another, then peered blearily over the edge of their straw nest. The kittens' mother, the spotted tabby cat, went to stick her nose out of the old barn door. The ginger kitten pattered after her, eager to see what was going on. He wriggled between his mother's front paws, staring out into the yard.

Mrs. Bowen was standing by the back of a van, next to two young women. One of the women opened up the doors and started to unload some odd-looking boxes. The van smelled strange, the kitten thought. He'd never smelled anything quite like it before. And what were those wire box things?

His mother was tense beside him, her whiskers pricked out as she watched what was going on. His brother and sisters were starting to meow and cry back in their nest, as they smelled the fear scents on their mother and the other older cats who were watching, too. They just didn't trust humans. The tabby cat backed into the barn so that her ginger baby wasn't between her paws anymore, and butted him hard with her nose.

He looked around in surprise. What was the matter? Why was she pushing him? Was it a game? Then he saw that her eyes were wide with fear, and the fur had risen all along her back. This was no game. She swiped the kitten with her paw, sending him sliding out into the yard, and then she hissed at him with her ears laid flat back against her head. It was quite clear what she was telling him to do.

Run!

The ginger kitten scooted quickly out of the barn door, heading for the old tractor. The tire had come away from the wheel, and the ginger kitten had found this wonderful hiding place while he was playing at jumping out on top of his sisters. There he waited, his heart thudding with fear, trying to figure out what was going on.

His mother had darted back into the barn to try to round up his brother and sisters, and some of the other cats were trying to make a run for it, too. But as soon as they'd seen that the cats knew they were there, the two women had quickly put a net around the barn door. Now they had on big gloves, and they were catching the cats with strange things that gripped them around the neck.

Ginger watched in horror as one by one his brother and sisters were caught and placed into wire cages. He could hear them meowing frantically as the cages were loaded into the van. Then one of the women walked right up to the tractor where he was hiding.

The kitten edged back as far as he could go, trembling. He didn't want the woman to see him, but now *he* couldn't see what was happening. Where were they taking his brother and sisters? Were they all in that horrible-smelling van? Had they caught his mother, too? He couldn't see! His tail thrashed from side to side as the woman walked past, searching—for him, maybe. Ginger curled himself into the tiniest ball, his eyes wide with fear.

"I just caught the last one. I'm glad I had my gloves, she was struggling like anything!" shouted a voice from across the farmyard. Ginger then listened as the woman walked away from the tractor and the van doors slammed shut.

As the van drove off, a small, bright pink nose peeked out from the wheel of the tractor. Ginger watched the van rattling out of the farm gate, carrying his brother and sisters away from him, and gave a miserable little meow. Should he try to follow them? But he was sure his mother hadn't been happy about where they were going. Where was his mother? Maybe she'd managed to find a hiding place, too? Perhaps she would come get him now that the people had left? Or should he try to find her?

Ginger crept out of his hiding place and started to search the farmyard. It smelled empty, and there was no sign of any other cats at all. But he couldn't believe that his mother had left him. She wouldn't! Even if they had caught her, she would have gotten away somehow.

He wandered around the outside of the barn, meowing sadly, and wishing she would come back soon, because he was getting hungry. Maybe she'd gone hunting for a nice mouse for his breakfast. Yes, that was probably it.

As the morning wore on, he got hungrier and hungrier. He searched around for his mother and meowed pitifully for her, but still she didn't come.

At last he went a little closer to the farmhouse, drawn by the smell from the garbage. Mrs. Bowen had been clearing out her fridge and cupboards, and there were some black plastic bags lying there. The kitten pawed at one of them hopefully and clawed a little hole, hooking out some old cheese. He nibbled at it. It wasn't very good, but it was better than nothing.

He ate all of it, his whiskers twitching at the strange taste. He wished the girl would come back and feed him some more of that delicious ham. He had been surprised when she pet him, but he'd liked it. If she came back now, he wouldn't be all on his own and she might pet him some more. Oh, if only *somebody* would come!

Rosie practically dragged Gran to the farmyard after school.

"All right, Rosie, all right! But we can't stay long. Mrs. Bowen is still busy packing. She's moving tomorrow. She won't want us bothering her today," Gran said firmly.

"I know, but I have to just find out about the kittens, whether the people came today. Mom said we might be able to stop in at the rescue center on the way home!" Rosie looked up at her gran with shining eyes. "If she likes him, we could even take him home this afternoon!"

Gran smiled. It was nice to see Rosie so excited, although she wasn't sure Rosie's mom would agree to a kitten.

Mrs. Bowen waved to them from the kitchen window. She was piling china carefully into a big box and looked a bit frazzled.

"Did they come?" Rosie asked her excitedly. "Did they take all the kittens to the rescue center?"

Mrs. Bowen smiled. "Oh, yes, dear. This morning."

"Have you got the address?" Rosie asked hopefully. "Mom says we can go look at the kittens—she might even let me keep one of them! The sweet little ginger one, you know?"

Mrs. Bowen wrote it down, and Rosie folded up the piece of paper and tucked it carefully in her pocket.

Mom had said she'd try to leave work early so they could go to the rescue center that evening, and now Rosie sat by Gran's front window, watching for her car. When her mom arrived at last, she dashed out to meet her.

"The kittens are at the rescue center! I've got the address, Mom. Come on, they're only open until six!" she cried.

Her mom laughed. "All right! But remember, Rosie, we're just looking. I know you hope we'll be taking that kitten home, but I still need to think about this. And anyway, I can't imagine we'll be allowed to take one of them yet. They'll need to be checked by a vet, to make sure they're healthy."

Rosie nodded. "But at least let's go see!" she pleaded.

Secretly, she was sure that as soon as her mom saw Ginger, she would give in. Maybe they wouldn't be able to take him home today, but they could still tell the rescue center people that they wanted him!

The animal shelter was in the next village. The woman at the reception desk knew about the kittens, and she smiled at Rosie's eager questions.

"I'm sure you can go see them," she said. "We wouldn't usually let people visit the kittens until we'd checked them over, but seeing as you already know them . . ." She led Rosie and her mom through to a room at the back, with large cat-runs in it.

Rosie spotted the tabby mother cat at once. She was prowling up and down the cage, looking anxious.

"Oh, she really doesn't like being shut in. And she must be upset that she's not with her kittens," Rosie said sadly.

The woman from the rescue center nodded. "I know. But because she's a feral cat, we need to separate her kittens from her now, before they get too old. It's so the kittens can get used to humans and to give them the best chance of settling in when they go to their new homes. They're in that cage at the end—want to see them?"

"Oh, yes . . . Come and see, Mom!" Rosie whispered, grabbing her mom's hand and pulling her along.

"Oh, they are sweet!" her mom agreed, peering through the wire. "Look at that little black one!"

But Rosie was staring anxiously into the cage. There were four kittens in the basket, curled up asleep—one black, and three tabbies. There was no little ginger kitten.

Ginger wasn't there!

Chapter Four

"Don't cry, Rosie," Mom said gently as they walked back to the car.

Rosie was trying not to cry, but there were just a few tears that she couldn't seem to stop. She was thinking about what could've happened at the farm when the cats were caught.

Why hadn't Ginger been with them?

He probably found a sneaky way out

of the barn and slipped away. But why? Perhaps he'd just been frightened of the rescue center people, but it was also possible that he had stayed behind at the farm to wait for her. Maybe he hadn't wanted to go with the other cats because of her, because she'd been feeding him and playing with him.

She had read about feral cats on the Internet and knew that they were good hunters, but Ginger was too young to hunt for himself. His mother would still have been catching food for her kittens and showing them how to chase the mice in the barns. Without her to feed him, he might starve. Rosie nodded firmly to herself. She had to go back to the farm. She just had to find him, however long it took.

Rosie was determined to stop and look for the kitten the next day, but she and Gran got a shock when they reached the farm. Gran had come another way to pick Rosie up from school, because she needed to go shopping, and they both stopped in surprise as they came close.

"Goodness, that went up quickly!" Gran exclaimed.

A huge wire fence was now surrounding the farmyard, covered in big signs about wearing hard hats, and no children allowed. It was a construction site already!

Rosie pressed her face up against the fence. The farmyard was deserted, with no sign of life at all.

"Can't we go in and look for him?" she asked Gran.

"No, Rosie, look—it says no one can go in." Gran sighed. "We'll just have to keep coming by and hope we spot him —or perhaps we could ask the workers to keep an eye out. There's no one here now, but I'm sure there will be soon, otherwise they wouldn't have bothered to put the fence up, would they?"

Gran was right. The next day, a couple of men in yellow hard hats were wandering around the construction site with a little machine that beeped, which Rosie and Gran guessed was some sort of measuring gadget. It took them awhile to catch the men's attention, but at last one of them came over.

"Yes?" he asked.

"Have you seen a kitten?" Rosie said nervously. "There were some cats here, and they were taken to a rescue center, but we think one of the kittens ran away and . . ." She trailed off. "We just wondered if you'd seen him? A ginger kitten?"

"No, sorry." The worker turned away. Rosie didn't dare call him back, even though she wanted to.

"Could you keep an eye out for him, please?" Gran called, and Rosie squeezed her hand gratefully. She'd wanted to ask that, too.

They continued walking, Rosie looking back sadly every so often. The fence looked like it went on forever.

"Don't give up hope, Rosie," Gran told her. "You never know."

But Rosie couldn't help feeling that her chances of finding Ginger were getting smaller and smaller. What if he had escaped before the fence went up? Maybe he wasn't there at all!

Ginger was hiding between two hay bales in the barn, peering out occasionally, and trembling as the men's heavy boots thumped past the door. Who were they? And why were they stamping and crashing around his home? He wished his mother and his brother and sisters would come back, but he was almost sure now that they were gone forever. If his mother had still been here, she would have come to find him by now, wouldn't she?

He had hidden in the barn when the men came to put the fence up, and he'd dashed back there again this morning when they returned. He didn't dare do more than poke his nose out occasionally to see if they'd gone. He was starving, and it was getting harder to find anything to eat in the garbage bags by the farmhouse.

There were voices outside now. Were more people coming? He shivered. He wanted the farm to go back to being quiet and safe like it was before. He listened miserably, but then his ears pricked up. He knew that voice. It was the girl! She was there! Maybe she'd known he was hungry and had brought him some more sandwiches? He edged nervously around the barn door, the fur on his back ruffling up.

The men were still there, and the girl was talking to one of them. If only they would go, he could run over to her. Perhaps she didn't know he was here. He meowed a tiny meow, hoping she would hear. But he didn't dare call more loudly in case the men saw him.

No! The girl was turning away. She was going!

Rosie walked sadly away down the road with Gran, leaving the kitten staring desperately after her.

The girl had left, and Ginger didn't know if she would come back. He felt so small and scared, and very, very alone. . . .

Chapter Five

On Friday Gran was waiting outside school for Rosie as usual. It was raining, and Rosie was taking awhile. She and Millie were among the last few to come out, and Millie had her arm around her friend.

"Rosie's really upset about Ginger," she explained to Rosie's grandma.

"I just don't think I'll ever see him

again," Rosie whispered sadly.

"You can't give up!" Millie said firmly.

Millie's mom had come over and was giving Rosie a concerned look. "Is everything okay, Millie?" she asked, and Millie explained about Ginger being missing.

"Poor little thing," her mom murmured. "Have you tried putting food out to tempt him, just in case he's still around?"

Rosie lifted her head. "No! No, we haven't, we should try that! Can we do that today, Gran? Oh no, I should have saved my sandwich for him!"

"You could buy some cat treats at the pet shop!" Millie suggested. "Sammy loves those, especially the salmon-flavored ones."

"Please!" Rosie begged. "I'll pay you back out of my allowance, Gran."

Gran smiled. "I think I can afford some cat treats. Come on."

"Oh, I wish I could come with you, but I've got dance class," Millie said. "I'd love to see him. I bet he'll come out for those cat treats."

"Thanks for the great idea," Rosie told her gratefully, and she and Gran set off to the pet shop.

"Call me and let me know if you see him!" Millie yelled after them, and Rosie turned back to wave. Millie had understood at once why she was so upset. She adored her fluffy white cat, Sammy. He'd been lost for a couple of days last year, and it had been awful.

Rosie chose the salmon treats, like Millie had suggested. Sammy was gorgeous and pudgy and liked his food —Ginger was sure to like them, too. Then they walked quickly over to the farm. From a long way down the road, they could hear banging and the rumbling sounds of big vehicles. Rosie and Gran exchanged a look and speeded up to see what was going on.

The farm looked so different. The construction workers were knocking down the old barn! A huge yellow digger was thundering past them on the other side of the fence—even Rosie felt scared by how big and loud it was. How would a kitten feel!

"Oh, no!" Rosie cried. "That's where the cats all used to sleep." She watched as the digger tore at the walls. She clung on to the wire fence, pressing her face against it so hard that she could feel the wires marking her forehead, and looked frantically around the building site. She still couldn't see the kitten.

"He's not there, is he?" she asked, her voice shaking. "You don't think he was in the barn when they—when they started pulling it down. . . ."

Gran stared through the fence at the workers and their machines, and sighed. "I don't know, Rosie. He could just be hidden away somewhere because he's frightened. It's so noisy, he might want to come out, but he doesn't dare." She put her arm around Rosie.

"Try the cat treats," she suggested gently. "Why don't you scatter a few through the fence? Maybe the smell will tempt him." She helped Rosie tear open the tough packet. "Goodness, I think he could smell that from miles away— they're very fishy, aren't they?"

The treats did smell very strong, and Rosie pushed a few through the wiring of the fence. Then they waited, watching the workers in their bright yellow vests and hard hats as they cleared away the broken pieces of wood that were all that was left of the kitten's home. But there was no sign of Ginger—no long white whiskers peeking out from behind a hay bale, no ginger tail flicking around the corner of the farmhouse. He was nowhere to be seen. After ten minutes of waiting and calling, Gran turned to Rosie.

"It's starting to rain, Rosie. We'd better go, but we'll try again. Maybe your mom will bring you over tomorrow or on Sunday. We won't give up."

Rosie nodded, feeling slightly better. She would never give up on Ginger.

Even though he was only across the farmyard, Ginger hadn't seen them. He was lurking under the abandoned tractor, shuddering each time the digger crashed and clanged through his old home. He had run out as soon as the builders had come into the barn, and had been hiding here ever since. He was wet, cold, and hungry, and now he didn't even have anywhere to sleep!

As the barn was flattened, Ginger came to a decision. This wasn't his home anymore. It hadn't been his home since his family had left—he realized now that his mother wasn't coming back. He needed to get away and find somewhere new.

Perhaps he could go find that nice girl with the sandwiches?

Rosie's mom took her back to the farm on Sunday, and they stood by the fence, calling for a while.

"Put some more cat treats down," Mom suggested. "Then at least he'll have something to eat."

Suddenly, Rosie gasped. "Mom, look!"

"What is it? Do you see him? I can't see anything." Mom peered through the fence.

"No, that's it, I can't see anything, that's the point! The cat treats I poked through the fence on Friday are gone!"

"Are you sure?" Mom asked.

"Definitely. I was right here, so they should be just on the other side of the fence. Ginger's been here; he's eaten them! Oh, Mom!" Rosie beamed at her, feeling so relieved. She bent down to empty some more cat treats out of the packet.

"Rosie, what's that?" Rosie looked up to see her mom pointing across the farmyard, down to the side of the farmhouse. "Can you see? It looks like something ginger, by the trash. . . ."

Rosie jumped to her feet. Mom was right. Slipping along the side of the farmhouse was a flash of gingery fur. It had to be him!

But then the creature slunk out farther into the yard, sniffing at the piles of wood from the barn. A gingery fox, with a bright white tail tip.

"Oh, no . . ." Rosie breathed. It wasn't very big, but compared to a tiny kitten it was huge. "It might hurt Ginger, and oh, Mom, I bet it was the fox who ate the cat treats!"

Mom sighed and nodded. "I'm afraid you could be right."

Sadly, they turned and walked away, Rosie blinking back tears. She had promised herself she wouldn't give up, but it was starting to look hopeless. . . .

That evening, Rosie's mom was determined to cheer her up. A television show they both liked was just about to start and Mom hurried upstairs to get her.

"Rosie!" she called, opening her bedroom door. "Are you coming downstairs? Oh, Rosie!"

Rosie was sitting huddled on the floor, leaning against her bed.

"What's the matter?" Mom asked, sitting down on the floor beside her. "You're crying!"

"I'll never see him again." Rosie sniffed. "What if he's hurt?" she whispered. "He might have been injured when the barn was knocked down. Maybe he got trapped somewhere. Maybe that fox has eaten him!" Tears rolled down Rosie's cheeks again.

"Ssshh, Rosie, don't say that." Mom hugged her close. "I don't think foxes normally attack cats. You're imagining the worst—the kitten might be fine. He's probably just staying hidden because he's frightened of the builders." She looked down, stroking Rosie's red hair. "You really love this kitten, don't you? You've tried so hard to make friends with him—Gran told me how patient you were, trying to get him to like you."

Rosie's mom hesitated. "Rosie, you know, we could try adopting one of the other kittens at the rescue center. . . . What about that pretty little black one?"

Rosie looked up, her eyes horrified and still teary. "We can't! We can't, Mom!"

"I mean, if we don't find Ginger," her mom explained gently.

Rosie shook her head. "He's special," she said in a quiet voice. "I think because he's ginger, too, like me. But it isn't just that. He seems so bright, and he's got so much bounce. . . . "

She twisted one of her red curls around her finger, deep in thought. It was true. Ginger *was* special. And if she couldn't have Ginger, she didn't want another kitten.

Chapter Six

Ginger had felt so brave when he decided to leave the farm and look for a new home. He had waited until all the people were long gone, and the farm was dark and quiet. He would find somewhere warm and comfortable. Maybe he'd even find that friendly girl with the food.

But he hadn't realized that the fence

went all around the farm. It was very high, and it was pinned down tight to the ground. He couldn't get out! Scratching and scrabbling at it didn't work, and when he tried climbing it, he fell. At last he had slunk miserably away to find a place to sleep. Eventually, he'd hidden himself in Mrs. Bowen's log pile, at the back of the farmhouse. It wasn't very comfortable, but it felt safe, far away from the noisy, smelly machines.

Most of the mice seemed to have been scared away by the men, too. He'd almost caught one once, but it had slipped into a hole at the last minute, leaving him worn out and hungrier than ever. It had seemed so easy when his mother did it. He'd found some rather fishy-tasting little round things by the fence over the last couple of days, but they hadn't filled him up. He'd seen a fox hanging around as well, and he had a feeling it had picked all the best pieces out of those trash bags, because there was nothing left.

Now he could feel himself growing weaker. Even though the rain leaked through into his log-pile nest and soaked him, he'd been grateful for it, as at least he wasn't thirsty. He'd been able to drink the water caught in the old buckets that were lying around the yard. But he needed more than water. He was sure the men had food. He'd smelled it, delicious smells like the sandwiches the girl used to bring him. They had been very good.

He had hoped she might come back, but she probably didn't like the big machines, either, he thought, as he drifted into a restless sleep.

Ginger was woken by the smell of ham sandwiches. A worker had stopped for lunch and was sitting on one of the big logs. The smell was irresistible. Ginger uncurled himself and crept out. The sandwiches were in an open box, lying next to the man. There was just one left, and a piece of wonderful pink ham trailed out of it. He had to have it. Ginger looked up at the man. He was staring across the yard, chewing slowly. He wouldn't notice, would he?

Ginger darted a paw into the box, hooking the bread with his claws.

"Hey! Get out of there, you!" The man swiped at him with his hand! Ginger shot away in terror, without even a morsel of bread to show for it. He raced up the tree that had been left standing in a corner of the yard by the fence, and crouched flat on one of the branches, quivering with terror. No one had ever tried to hit him before. He looked down fearfully, digging his claws into the bark. He had never climbed a tree before, either, but instinct had taken him to the safest place. The man hadn't followed him.

Ginger stayed there for hours, too scared to move. By the middle of the afternoon, he felt it might be safe to come down from the tree. It wasn't as easy as going up had been. He hadn't really *thought* about going up, he'd just done it. He looked down from his branch—the ground seemed so far away. . . . He was stuck!

Rosie only got through school that day because Millie kept nudging her, reminding her that Mrs. Wilkinson was watching. Rosie would manage to listen or concentrate on what she was supposed to be doing for about five minutes, before she started thinking about Ginger again.

Millie was coming back to Gran's for dinner today, and they were planning to look for Ginger together. Rosie was glad—Millie was so enthusiastic about looking for him. Rosie had been disappointed so many times, it was hard to keep her hopes up.

Millie jogged ahead as they came up to the farm. "Wow! It really is a construction site. Oh, Rosie, poor Ginger. He must be really scared with all those people around, and those great big diggers. It's so noisy!"

Rosie nodded sadly and looked wearily through the fence into the farmyard. It looked so different now, with the barn gone and the yard covered in piles of rubble. She wasn't expecting to see anything. But what was that in the big tree over there? Rosie peered through the wire fence and grabbed Millie's sleeve.

"Millie! Gran! Look! Is that a cat in

the tree? On that branch, there. No, no, there, look!"

A flash of ginger fur showed among the yellowing leaves. It was hard to see if it was a cat, but *something* was moving.

"You could be right. . . ." Millie murmured doubtfully. "I can't quite see."

Gran was squinting through the fence at the tree. "I can't tell, either. . . ."

"I am right! I know I am!" Rosie looked at them eagerly. "He's there, he really is. Yes, I can see his stripes! Oh, I can't believe it, I'd almost given up. Ginger! Ginger! I don't think he can hear me, with all this noise." She frowned. "Oh, Gran, he must be so scared with all this going on. We have to get him out, we just have to!"

She dashed along the fence to the gate, with Millie racing after her, and shouted to one of the men walking by. "Hey! Excuse me! Over here, please listen!"

But the man just walked past, pushing a wheelbarrow. He didn't even look at Rosie and Millie. Rosie rattled the gate, but no one seemed to hear her, the site was too noisy.

Gran came up, looking anxious. "Rosie, calm down!"

"I can't make anyone listen!" Rosie looked at her wildly. "They have to let us in so we can go get him!"

Gran pulled them gently away from the gate. "Girls, come back, it's a building site, I don't think they'll let us go in. Sshh, look, that man's coming out. We'll ask him." Gran smiled politely at the worker, who was giving them a curious look.

"Excuse me, but have you seen a ginger kitten around at all? He used to live on the farm, and he's disappeared. We think we might have just seen him in that tree."

The worker shook his head. He didn't look very interested. "No cats, sorry," he said, starting to shut the gate.

"He *is* there!" Rosie cried. "We just saw him, we know he's there. You've knocked down his home, you might've hurt him! You have to let us find him!"

The worker looked confused, and Gran hugged Rosie tight. "Calm down, Rosie. Look, I'm sorry, the girls are very worried about the kitten. We really do think we saw him a minute ago. Could you please just keep an eye out for him?" She pulled an old receipt out of her bag and scribbled on it. "This is my phone number. If you could call us if you see him, we'd be so grateful."

The man took the note and stuffed it into the pocket of his reflective vest. Then he locked the gate and walked off. Rosie watched him go, tears running down her nose. She was pretty sure he'd never look at the note again.

Gran walked Rosie and Millie away from the gate. She was worried the builders might get annoyed and tell them to stop hanging around.

From high up in the tree, Ginger had heard the voices. It was the girl! The one with the food, who did the petting. She'd come back for him. He was sure that was why she was there. He tried desperately to scrabble down the tree trunk.

But now she was going! She couldn't have seen him. He meowed frantically, *Please wait!* But no one heard him. He took a flying leap from halfway down the tree trunk and raced over to the fence.

Come back! Come back! I'm here!

But it was too late.

Chapter Seven

When they got back to Gran's house, she made Millie and Rosie sit down and have a glass of juice.

"You mustn't get so upset, Rosie!" Gran said. "You can't help that kitten if you're shouting at people and getting into trouble, can you?"

Rosie sighed and shook her head. Gran was right. "I just don't think he was even listening, Gran," she said sadly. "That's why I was so imptient. That man just said no cats, without even thinking about it!"

"But you saw him, Rosie!" Millie put in. "He's still there—that's really good news! That was your ginger kitten, wasn't it?"

Rosie smiled at last. "I'm sure, really sure. I could see his stripy fur through the leaves. He was up in that tree, I know he was. I wish he'd heard me, but it was just so noisy. I bet he would have come down, to see if I had sandwiches again." She frowned. "I hope he wasn't stuck; that tree's enormous."

"Well, all we can do is go again tomorrow. As long as we're back in time for your mom to pick you up, I don't mind how long we stay. If we're there when the workers have left and it's quiet, then it'll be easier." Gran smiled. "If he's there, we'll find him."

"Couldn't we go back now?" Rosie pleaded. "I'm not sure I can wait until tomorrow. . . ."

Gran shook her head. "It's getting late now and you both still need to have dinner. We can go right after school tomorrow."

"Okay," Rosie sighed.

Ginger sat by the fence and howled. She'd been here, and he'd missed her! He scratched desperately at the fence, hoping to chase after the girl, but it didn't budge at all. He was still trapped.

He trailed sadly back to the woodpile, avoiding the builders. At least she had come back. Maybe she'd come again tomorrow?

Rosie raced along the road, hardly hearing Gran calling to her to slow down. She was desperate to get to the farm and see if Ginger was still there. At last she reached the fence by the tree where Ginger had been yesterday. She wound her fingers through the wire, gazing hopefully up at the tree. There was no glint of ginger fur. Rosie sighed. Still, she couldn't expect him to be in exactly the same place he was yesterday; that would be silly.

He's there, she told herself firmly. *You just need to look.*

Rosie tiptoed along the fence, trying to peer through. The awful thing was, Ginger might be asleep somewhere, just out of sight! She could miss him so easily.

Suddenly, Rosie gasped. It was as though all her breath had disappeared. He was there! Keeping so still that she hadn't spotted him at first. He was crouched under the giant wheel of the old tractor, where she used to sit to tempt him with sandwiches. His ears were laid back, and he was watching the workers. Rosie's heart thudded miserably as she saw how thin he was getting.

Rosie crouched down by the fence. "Ginger!" she whispered, not wanting to scare him, but of course he didn't hear her. She tried again, a little louder, and his ears twitched.

"Ginger!" Rosie waved to him as well this time, and she saw his eyes widen. He'd seen her! He stood up slowly, cautiously, and crept across the yard toward her, moving one paw at a time and glancing around fearfully.

Rosie's eyes filled with tears as she saw how scared he was. "Hey, Ginger!" she whispered gently as he stopped a foot or so from the fence.

He stood hesitantly, staring at her, and gave a very small meow. Had the girl come back for him?

"Oh, Ginger, I'm so glad to see you!" Rosie murmured. "Are you all right? You look okay, just really thin." She giggled. "I don't know why I'm asking you all these questions, it isn't as if you can answer. . . ." Very slowly, Rosie reached into her school bag. "Look, I've got your favorite. . . ." She opened up her lunch box, pulling out the sandwich she'd saved. "Yummy ham, Ginger, come and see!"

Ginger ran toward her. She *had* come back! And she'd brought food. He was still nervous, but she'd always been so gentle, and the food just smelled too good to resist. Ginger had gotten used to Rosie feeding him, and he'd missed her. He sat on the other side of the fence and meowed hopefully.

"Here you go, it's okay," Rosie said, laughing and passing pieces of sandwich through the fence. Ginger gobbled them down eagerly. "You look like you haven't eaten for a week," Rosie told him. Her eyes widened. "Actually, it *has* been a week, hasn't it? You must be starved. Here, have some more."

"Rosie, I can't believe you've already found him! I won't come closer in case I frighten him off, all right? I'll just stay back here." Gran leaned against the fence on the other side of the road, watching Rosie and the kitten.

Ginger finished the sandwich and sniffed the ground, looking for crumbs. The sandwich had helped, but he still felt hungry. He wondered if the girl had any more. He looked at her uncertainly and edged forward, closer and closer still. At last he was right up against the fence, sniffing at Rosie's fingers. He even licked them, in case she tasted like ham, but she didn't.

Rosie giggled—his tongue was tickly—and scratched him behind the ears. She could only just reach—the holes in the fence were too small for her whole hand to go through. "How are we going to get you out?" Rosie muttered as she stroked Ginger's head with one finger.

He ducked his head shyly, rubbing himself against the wire. It was warm and sunny, he had been fed, and now someone he liked was petting him. He closed his eyes and started to purr very quietly, his tiny chest buzzing.

Rosie could feel him trembling with the purr as he leaned against the wire, letting her stroke him all over. She almost felt like purring herself, and a huge smile spread over her face.

"He's purring!" she hissed to Gran in a loud whisper. Rosie was just starting to wonder if she should call to a nearby worker, and ask him to pick Ginger up and bring him out to her. It wouldn't take him long, and they couldn't *want* a kitten getting in their way. . . .

Then a man tripped and dropped the bucket he was carrying. It hit the ground with a huge clang. Ginger leaped into the air in fright, and Rosie jumped, her heart thumping.

Ginger had disappeared, streaking across the yard in a panic, and Rosie looked anxiously around for him, clinging sadly to the wire fence. He had trusted her—he'd actually been enjoying her petting him, and now all that good work was for nothing! She sighed hopelessly. Ginger was so nervous. It wasn't his fault, but he was never going to let one of the workers pick him up. He ran away from the women from the rescue center, and that was before he'd had a week of scary construction workers invading his home.

Ginger would let her feed him and pet him. But she was on one side of the fence, and he was on the other. How was she ever going to get him out?

Chapter Eight

"Oh, Rosie, he was so close!" Gran came hurrying over, her face stricken. "That was such bad luck. He really seemed to be trusting you." She shook her head. "I just can't believe how patient you've been with him. You deserve to have him, Rosie, you really do."

Rosie gave her a grateful hug.

"Well, what are we going to do now?" Gran wondered. "How on earth are we going to get him out? He's too frightened to let anyone pick him up— you might be able to do it, but those workers can't let you go on the site, even if they wanted to. If you hurt yourself, they could be in real trouble. I suppose we're just going to have to call the rescue center and get them to do it."

Rosie nodded. "I didn't think about the rescue center people coming back. They'd probably have to use a net or a cage or something, wouldn't they?" She shuddered. "I suppose it's better than staying where he is. It's really dangerous here. But he'll be terrified and he might run away from them again. . . . Oh, Gran, there's got to be a better way!" She sat down on the grass, thinking hard. "Well, I can't go in, so he's got to come out, right? But I just don't see how—this fence is like a prison, even for a cat."

Gran sighed. "I've a feeling we're going to be here for a while, aren't we?" She patted Rosie on the shoulder. "You stay here and watch for him. I'll run home and make us some sandwiches. I won't be long." Rosie looked up suddenly. "Don't worry, Rosie, I'll bring some more ham for Ginger as well. But if we do catch that kitten, he's going to have to learn to like something other than the most expensive ham. . . ."

Rosie watched her walk slowly off down the road. She was so lucky having Gran. For one thing, if Gran didn't watch her after school, she'd never even have met Ginger. But mostly because Gran was never in a rush. She didn't mind spending an hour sitting outside a construction site, watching for a kitten. That was pretty special.

Rosie turned back to the fence and stared at it hopelessly. If only she could climb over it! The workers were starting to leave now. Once they'd left, no one would see. . . . But the fence was so high, and Gran would be really upset with her. She'd trusted Rosie to be sensible, leaving her here. Rosie couldn't let her down.

Rosie shook the fence, making it rattle. It was even taller than the one at school, around the playing field. Then she stopped and stared at the fence thoughtfully. The one at school had holes in it, where people had leaned on it over the years, and one place where some of the boys in the grade above her had decided to dig a tunnel underneath while they were bored at recess. She couldn't get *over* the fence, but maybe she could get *under* it. Or at least the kitten could. . . .

She crouched down again and peered at the base of the fence. It ran along the ground, and it was held tightly between posts, so there were no gaps—yet. Rosie started to hunt for a likely place. Oh! Yes, here, a couple of posts along . . . Something had already done half the job for her. Maybe that fox they'd seen before. Whatever it was had burrowed a hole a few inches deep under the fence before it gave up.

Rosie lifted the fence carefully. She was pretty sure that Ginger could fit under there, but she'd better dig it out some more, just to be certain. Rosie found a big stone and started to scrape the earth away as fast as she could, looking up every so often to check for Ginger.

The farm was quiet. Ginger's ears and whiskers stopped their panicky twitching at last, and he poked his nose out from under the black tarp where he'd dashed after that huge bang.

No noise of diggers, no rumbling wheels, no men shouting. They were gone. It should be safe now. He slid out, still listening carefully. There was an odd scritch-scratching noise coming from across the yard. It wasn't the men. Was it that fox who'd been stealing from his garbage cans? He'd seen it again the other night.

There was no smell now, so it couldn't be a fox. He padded slowly out into the yard, following the noise. It sounded like something was digging under the fence; maybe it *was* that fox. The fur rose up on Ginger's back. The sooner he got out of here, the better. He crept around the back of the tractor and took a quick look over at the fence.

It was her! The girl! She was still there! The noise hadn't scared her away. And she was digging under the fence. Was she trying to come in?

Ginger gave a hopeful meow, and crept across the yard toward her, glancing around occasionally, just in case.

Rosie dropped the stone. "Ginger!" She sat up on her heels eagerly, catching hold of the fence to look through the wire, and Ginger paused, scared by the sudden movement. "Oh, I'm sorry. . . ." She edged back on her knees, leaving a little space between herself and the fence. "I didn't mean to scare you, Ginger. I was just so glad to see you! Look!" Rosie dug the last tiny handful of fishy cat treats out of the packet that she'd been keeping in her school bag, and scattered them for Ginger—on her side of the fence.

"Come on, Ginger. . . . please. . . ."

The tiny kitten sniffed thoughtfully. The smell was familiar. Those strange round things he'd found before! They were from the girl, too? Well, he preferred ham sandwiches, but he wouldn't complain. Still, he had to climb under the fence to get them.

He padded closer, peering through the hole. It seemed big enough. And he'd been hoping to find the girl, and a way out. Now she had made him one. Ginger stared up at Rosie, his big green eyes hopeful, and almost trusting. He would do it.

Rosie stared back, her eyes hopeful, too, and pleading, desperate for him to trust her. "Hey, little one," she whispered. "Come on. . . ."

Ginger crouched down, and started to wriggle under the fence, the wire just skimming the fur on his back. He popped out on the other side, shook himself, and sneezed from the dust. Then he eyed the cat treats eagerly.

"Go on, they're for you!" Rosie reassured him, and Ginger gobbled them up, a curious expression on his face. Such an odd flavor. But he could get used to it. He licked his whiskers to make sure he hadn't missed anything, and looked up at Rosie. Then he put one tiny paw on her knee and meowed. *More?*

"Are you still hungry?" Rosie smiled. "You could come back to Gran's with me. . . . She's making ham sandwiches, your favorite." She stood up very slowly and stepped backward. "You coming? Hmmm? Coming, Ginger?"

And Ginger stepped out after her, his tail waving, following her home.

Lost in the Snow

Fluff is desperate for a home of her own and Ella really wants to adopt her, but Ella's mother says no. What happens to a kitten that nobody wants?

Lost in the Storm

Fluff loves being outside and playing in the snow. But a blizzard sets in and she can't find her way home!

Alfie All Alone

Evie loves her puppy Alfie, but when her family has a new baby, nobody has much time to play with the poor dog.

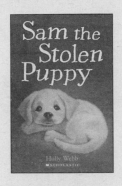

Sam the Stolen Puppy

Sam is a great puppy and when he is stolen from Emily's yard, she is determined to get her dog back.

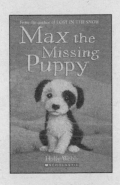

Max the Missing Puppy

Max loves to play with Molly so much that he goes out looking for her when she is at school. Will he be able to find his way back home?

Sky the Unwanted Kitten

Lucy doesn't want to move, so her parents buy her a kitten. But Lucy ignores Sky, who can't figure out why her new girl won't play with her.

Animal Rescue
Tina Nolan

Abandoned . . . lost . . . neglected?
There's always a home at Animal Magic!

In a perfect world, there'd be no need
for Animal Magic. But Eva and Karl
Harrison, who live at the animal rescue
center with their parents, know that life
isn't perfect. Every day there's a new
arrival in need of their help!

Tina Nolan

Honey

The unwanted puppy

SCHOLASTIC

Tina Nolan

Charlie

The home-alone kitten

SCHOLASTIC

Tina Nolan

Merlin

The homeless foal

SCHOLASTIC

Tina Nolan

Rusty

The injured fox cub

SCHOLASTIC

Tina Nolan

Holly

The doorstep puppy

SCHOLASTIC

Run, fly, or swim down to Grace's Pet Shop.

Lottie is happy to spend her time talking to the animals in her uncle's pet shop. Then one day, to her surprise, the animals start to talk back!

School is definitely more fun now that Lottie has best friend, Ruby. But what will her new friend do if she finds out Lottie has magical powers?

A new neighbor is in town, with magic stronger than Lottie's and a mind to make trouble. Lucky for Lottie, the pet shop's newest resident, Giles the hamster, is ready to help.

Lottie has discovered an unhappy rabbit at a dingy pet shop. He seems to have budding magical abilities and Lottie is determined to rescue him!

Magic is everywhere and all the animals can talk!

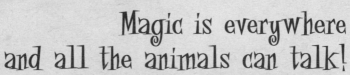

THE PUPPY PLACE

SO MANY PERFECT PUPPIES – COLLECT THEM ALL!